AN UNEXPECTED JOURNEY

AADIYA CHAUHAN

BlueRoseONE.com
Stories Matter
NewDelhi • London

BLUEROSE PUBLISHERS
India | U.K.

For permissions requests or inquiries regarding this publication, please contact:

BLUEROSE PUBLISHERS
www.BlueRoseONE.com
info@bluerosepublishers.com
+91 8882 898 898
+4407342408967

ISBN: 978-93-5819-133-2

Cover design: Shivam
Typesetting: Namrata Saini

First Edition: September 2023

About the Author

Aadiya Chauhan is a charming, fun-loving, 14-year-old teenage girl. When she was 3, she started learning SKATES; at 5, she started learning the art of BHARATNATTYAM (one of the supreme Indian dance forms) and at 10 she started writing small stories and poems, just for fun. One of her stories got recognition at the school, which inspired her to write a book and become an author.

Aadiya is a SKETCH ARTIST and currently learning the art of pencil shading and digital are. All the pictures in the book are designed by Aadiya.

Picking Fiction & Fantasy as her genre, she started researching the subject by reading books and watching content on TV, OTT & Internet. Her first book, **'HEROES &**

VILLAINS', was published in the year 2022, when she was 13 years.

Aadiya hails from India, a diverse and culturally rich country, which is one of the most ancient civilizations in the world. India is a country of great ancient scholars like Chanakya, Aryabhata, and the home of the first residential university of the world... 'Nalanda'. A densely populated secular country with over 400 languages, 2000 dialects, and a universe of heritage.

Aadiya belongs to an educated family, and she aspires to achieve profound knowledge to pursue her dream of becoming an author of repute.

'AN UNEXPECTED JOURNEY' is her second book and we hope you will like her fictional work.

Acknowledgement

I would like to take this opportunity to thank everyone who helped me start, write, and publish my second book. I'd first like to thank my mother, Dadi, father, and my beloved younger sister for encouraging me continuously in my efforts to become an author. I love you all so, so much!!!

Special thanks to my Mom for helping me in making the sketches expressive.

I'd also like to thank the Team of BlueRose Publishers for showing faith in my abilities and making sure my book reaches your hands.

Finally, I'd like to thank you dear reader for picking up my book and if at all you liked it.

With warm regards
Aadiya Chauhan
ascaadiya@gmail.com
https://aadiyachauhan.in

About the book

It was the end of summer break, end of a wonderful trip, before...

Sally Manter and her 4 brothers- E-jay, Chris, Sam and Jack almost met with an accident and almost drowned in the ocean...

But now they're lost trying to find a way back home but with some magical twists...

'AN UNEXPECTED JOURNEY' awaits...

Here's how the story unveils...

Contents

Ocean and Beach 1

An abnormaler place 9

The Forest 17

A normaler place 32

Crasioda 38

Questions and answers 44

Can we stop this conversation already? 50

Walking to the spaceship 53

Lost 56

The fight 60

Another tree 65

How Jack's mind works 69

There we go again 75

Going back 78

Ocean and Beach

I almost fell asleep as the cold wind blew through my face in the caravan. Today was the last day of our trip. It had been so good. Camping, amusement park, beaches; but I guess everything has to come an end, right?

But just guess what's waiting for me? by two more days my summer vacation was ending, ***Plus,*** I hadn't even started my holiday homework; I don't even know what it is. Honestly though, you can't blame me, I hardly had time to think about *anything* before today's return journey.

I have four brothers and I'm the second youngest.

Let's start off with Jack because... I think, talking about him first is important because, if I don't, you'll pretty much forget that he even was here. He is 11, and pretty short. He has brown eyes like all of us and black hairs that are always covering his whole face. He really doesn't do anything except read books from time to time or go through his phone. I guess this made it clear that he is really, really shy and doesn't talk a lot.

Then there's Sam. He's sixteen and one of the ***BIGGEST*** nerds on the planet. That guy doesn't even need to touch a book before exam and will still manage to get A+. But he still will be with a book in his arms 24/7 and I mean textbooks, not novels or whatever, *textbooks!* He actually enjoys reading them. Anyway, he has black hairs, round glasses over his brown eyes. He is also a mood spoiler when it comes to jokes. As boring as he is, sometimes he's the only sensible person you'll find.

Chris, *ugh,* Chris, he is a whole different story. He is 18 and honestly, he thinks he's the creator of the world or something. He has jet-black hairs and brown eyes. As much as I hate to admit it, he actually looks way better than any person I've ever seen (half the reason he considers himself the creator of the world) which I can't disagree even if I try but that's pretty much all about him. In a few months he will graduate from high school but it doesn't look like he has any plans for future at all. Yes, he is the most annoying one even though the competition is tough.

Then there's E-jay, he's like substitute mom even though, he's like just a year older than Chris. He had moved out 2 years ago because he got admission in a big university abroad early but he keeps visiting us from time to time. He is what parents call the perfect child. He has brown eyes and brown hairs. Even though he's very protective (just what makes him annoying) he'd be the most understanding out of everyone.

All of us are very, very different from each other. Although, if there's one thing we have in common, it's the fact that we all ***love*** travelling. Wait... I forgot to introduce myself, didn't I? Well, hi guys I'm Sally, and I'm 14 and I guess you could remember me as the brave one in the group. All my brothers are scared of literally everything. I have brown hairs (Me and E-jay are the only ones with brown hairs) and brown eyes.

Now, when I was 11, E-jay had got a driving license, and since then every summer vacation he takes us to multiple places in our family caravan. It's usually fun exploring the country. We usually take long brakes because E-jay's the only one with a driving license ... Well, this time even Chris should have had his driving license, but... he has failed the driving test not once or twice but like so many times that I've actually lost count. It's probably because he simply can't concentrate on anything for more than 3 secs and as far as I know driving needs concentration. Before E-jay had got his driving license, we did go to a lot of places during summer vacations but they were always a one-day trip like a water park or something on Sundays. This is because my mom and dad own one of the biggest companies in all of Australia and they've always been too busy, so they can't really afford to take leaves. That is why when E-jay gave this idea to mom and dad, they felt happy that all of us could finally enjoy our vacations.

We were going alongside the sea in port McDonnell when we stopped at a restaurant to have food. After we were done eating, E-jay turned to Chris, "You wanna try to drive for a while?"

I suddenly was too aware about this all.

"E-jay, are you *okay??*" I said before Chris could say anything. "You know how he drives."

"Um..." Chris said rather coldly sipping his smoothie with no emotion on his face. "Who told you to reply for me?"

He looked up.

"So would you rather have all of us dead by your driving? You're never gonna learn driving!" I said a little loud so he won't cut-short my point.

"I think we should let Chris drive." Jack said.

"Jack, let us talk." I said.

"Okay, don't you think we need to support him as family, Sally?" E-jay said trying to sound calm before this could turn into a fight. Except it already had.

"Yeah", Sam said, who was just listening till now knowing that we won't make it home if we trust his driving. "I don't know about anyone else but if he drives, I'm taking a cab home."

"Sam." E-jay said his face annoyed.

"Who are you to interrupt anyway, huh?" Chris said. Since the last time he spoke anything, he just had his eyes narrowed, observing while sipping his smoothie. "You're sixteen, you can't drive either."

"Okay, I get the point," Sam said sarcastically standing up from his chair. "I should know how to drive 'cuz I've been learning to drive for 3 weeks and you for 2 years. Why? 'Cuz 3 is bigger than 2"

"Stop it!" E-jay said getting up from his chair. "Chris is driving and that's final! And Sam, sit down."

"E-jay, seriously?" I said.

"Sally, I'm not hearing it." E-jay said this with his 'I'm your big brother, obey me' type of voice.

I gave up. I know he won't listen after 'I'm not hearing it'. *Fine,* I thought, *don't.* I can't believe he would do this again. I mean, he knows how Chris and one of his friends almost met with an accident last time Chris was driving, doesn't he? I had once sat in the car while he was driving and I was legit shaking by the time I got off. Me, the girl who's *said*(emphasis on 'said') to be afraid of nothing was *shaking* after coming out of his car.

Whatever, we sat in the car and Chris started driving. He started driving. I was holding my breath making sure to check nothing is in the way, holding my breath every time another car was passing. I calmed down a little as time moved. I have to say, he *had* improved a lot since the last time I made the mistake of sitting in the car as he drove. He was more patient, and he was actually listening to E-jay and correcting the faults he made. I almost felt impressed before...

"Not so bad after all, huh?" Chris screamed from the driving seat flipping his hairs. I ignored him, I mean even if he did improve, it is only natural for anyone (anyone, that is except E-jay) to feel a red-light alert when Chris is driving if they've ever even *seen* him drive before.

I still wasn't really not on guard, though. Anything could happen at any time and I needed to make sure that my hand was right on the door handle for any case (even though I know it won't do any good). After a while though, I fell asleep. I was too tired not to.

BOOM! -is the first thing I hear as I jerk awake. *I was wrong.* -is the first thing, I think. *I was so terribly wrong!* I looked at Chris to see his leg on the accelerator as E-jay screamed at him to take his leg off the accelerator. He did that in panic.

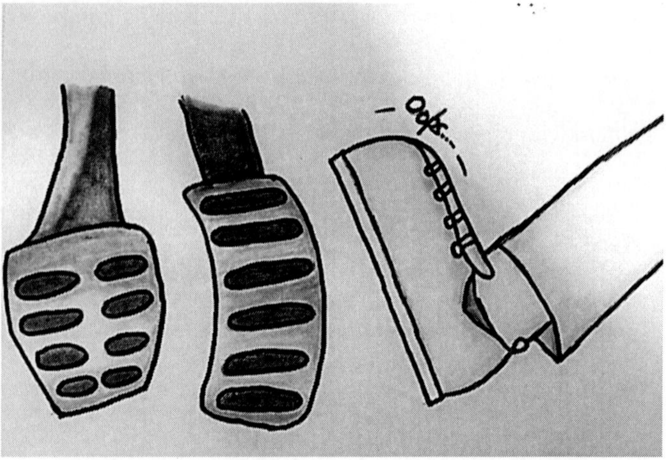

He confused break with accelerator?

Even in all this panic, all I could think of, was that even I know the difference between a break and an accelerator.

Everyone was screaming and everything was chaos. Our caravan was practically flying towards the ocean after it jerked off the slope. We were falling on the deep side. I tried to think of something and realized all in split second- *windows*- they will help us escape. I opened my window in a rush as I heard a loud a splash!

An Abnormaler Place

I saw the blue ocean swallowing us inside itself. I saw water quickly filling in because my window was open. Although, window being opened wasn't a bad thing at all. It meant we could escape easily.

Whoosh! I heard a sudden sound way different from the noise of the ocean in my ears and I swear, I saw the ocean grow dark all of a sudden.

There was no time to think, I turned towards the backseat, grabbed jack's hand (the only one among us who couldn't swim) and got out of my window gesturing to everyone else to do the same and started swimming upwards.

It was way harder to reach upwards than I had thought it would be. My legs were moving fast but it was hard to fight for oxygen especially in the panic in my mind. I swam and swam till I swooshed up. I imagined seeing the beach somewhere near but I saw something else, the water was *grey* in colour, an unusual metallic *grey* and I looked up only to realize that so was the sky. That was weird but I didn't give it a lot of thought because of the situation, but I did pay attention to the beach which had shifted further away than I would have expected, it was around half a kilometer away, how did Chris even manage to push the caravan this far?

I stopped thinking much about it because right now, my life's mission seemed to be to reach back to the beach. I glanced down in water, which was surprisingly very clear and tried to make out the rest of them. I only realized ow that somehow my eyes were not burning as they should. Living by the beachside for my whole life, I've always made sure not to go to ocean water without my swim glasses on, or else my eyes would burn terribly. I looked down to see three figures swimming up. I should've started swimming but I needed to make sure they were okay, they came up, gradually. After this I started pushing myself and Jack towards the shore.

I swam towards the shore, breathing with difficulty. It wasn't that hard though, somehow, I knew just how to push myself right. My legs were slowly giving up and as much as I really didn't want it to, it was hard holding on to Jack. I reached the shore in around the longest ten minutes of my life. I reached back to the beach and that's when I actually realized something was really, really, wrong.

It wasn't the rocky beach I remembered (also, I realized the 'weirdity' of what I'd already realized while I was swimming), rather it wasn't like any beach I could ever think of.........

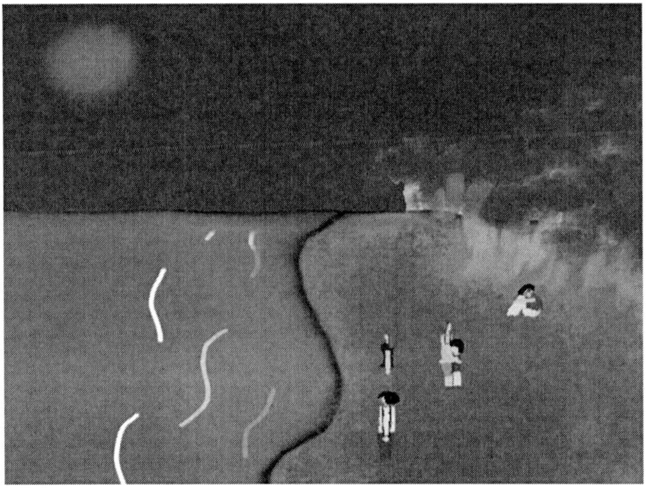

It had *purple* sand. The ocean was metallic grey and I looked at the sky just to realize that it was just as grey as the water.

The others slowly started coming to the shore, and before I even had a chance to say anything about anything to anyone, Chris freaked out and screamed.

"WHAT IS THIS??" He screamed and started running around the beach to reach nowhere with his eyes wide and hands in the air.

"Stop screaming." I said irritated. "It's all your fault anyway."

Chris was way too scared to say anything and continued his running.

"Where are we?" Jack asked.

"How am I supposed to know?" I said louder than I wanted to.

"I think we're not where we left from." E-jay said.

"Oh, I had no clue." I sighed sarcastically. "Look who just woke up from sleep. Were you sleeping even when I told you not to let Chris drive??!!" my voice had started out normal but turned into a scream by the end.

Chris got up to reply, "Ok, now, stop blaming me-" "You. Dare. Speak. Another word. I'm way too angry to speak to *you* of all people right now." This was so typical me, screaming at the people I'm angry at and not even talking to the people I'm really angry at.

"Tell me E-jay." I said my angry sarcasm increasing with each word. "What will the big bro do now, huh? I mean you would know where we are, right? *Help us!* We're so scared!"

E-jay looked down. He seemed genuinely guilty and I wasn't really helping it and felt like I said too much, but his guilt won't change the fact that we were on a weird creepy island which looked someone added the first random colours, they could find in it. I turned around. There was a forest behind us. At least it looked closest near to a forest; the trees had large *green* trunks and *brown* leaves, broad and shaped like spilled water.

What's going on?

Wait, maybe it was a really realistic movie set or something. That could explain most of the weird things that happened to us till now. Who am I kidding? No movie set would be *this* realistic.

Stop. I told myself. Think of something else. Don't freak out on this. I mean this is like a movie. If we manage to get out maybe there'd actually be a movie on this. I laughed at the thought, but if we had planned to come here, I'm pretty sure I'd be less creeped out by this. I wasn't like the *others,* I *wasn't* freaked out or scared; I was just confused how we could end up here. I'll put this place to my checklist to come to when I grow up. because I don't wanna explore it with everyone else trying not to scream. I sighed.

Finally, I asked Sam because I couldn't think of asking anyone else, "Any ideas on how do we get out of here?"

That's when I noticed Sam was sitting far away from the waves near the forest, his head on his knees, shaking.

"Are you okay?" I asked genuinely concerned but still trying not to laugh.

"No" he said straightforward. "This place is weird. I'm scared."

"Sam, get up." I replied. I told you; my brothers are scared of literally everything.

"Anyone, who could save their phone?" I asked when he didn't listen to me. "Anyone?"

"How does it matter? There's no signal." Chris said matter-of-factly.

I ignored him. I just wasn't liking him talk right now. Everyone checked their pockets.

"I have it." E-jay said after checking his pocket. "But seriously, what will you do with it? We can't call mom or dad or something."

"I had no idea." I said sarcastically while taking his phone.

To be honest, I really didn't know what I could do with this. And it wasn't as if I didn't know that there was no signal, but there could be *something* that could help that didn't need internet. I mean, it can't be completely no help.

After around 15 minutes of analyzing, I gave up, this phone *was* absolutely no help, except the compass app. Time to be traditional and use compass to guide our way.

We fell southwards to reach here, so logically, we'll have to go north to reach back, but for some weird reason north wasn't in the direction from where we came, north was towards the forest. I think we would have to go in the forest after all, I mean there could be tribal people who could lend us a boat, or......... a venomous snake, yep, keep going brain, good job! Try to warn me not to use the only option we have.

I told everyone that we should go in the forest and we slowly headed towards the forest. Everyone followed me like obedient kids. I was the only one who was still in the right state of mind here. I didn't want everyone to come inside the forest though, I'm scared they might do something stupid, but leaving them alone anywhere was definitely more dangerous than taking them in the forest with me. Plus, E-jay wouldn't have let me go alone anyways and he knows I wouldn't consider denying. I know how overprotective he gets all the time but I get it. At least, right now I do, considering how overprotective I'm getting myself.

The Forest

As we went in the forest, I was ahead of everyone-I mean, obviously- and I managed to realize that this place was way weirder than I could've thought.

"The trees have a really smooth texture here." Jack said.

"Who cares?" I replied.

Sam took his hand over the tree trunk to check the texture feeling amazed. It felt smooth as iron.

"If we take pictures of this place, we could be a big scientific and geographic revolution." He spoke. Then looked at E-jay and said "Give me your phone."

"I'm pretty sure this place is already discovered." I said and then looked at him and sort of laughed while saying, "Just that you didn't know about it."

He ignored it and glanced up and reached out to take one of the leaves, only to find ... a spider sitting over them! If it was a spider, that is.

"Oh, my god!" Sam screamed almost falling on Chris who was behind him.

When I looked at the spider, it was huge almost more than the size of my face, but the only thing spider about it was its legs and the fact that it was on a web. It looked as if someone had pasted 8 spider legs on a bird. It also had stripes all over it, yellow and blue.

"Woah." I said, my eyes wide and amazed. This was so amazing. Weird too, but amazing.

Sam took a pic of that too. Finding weird creatures didn't really end there though. As we walked, we found many such creatures who looked like a mixture of a few different animals. There was a rabbit with a cat face and dog ears. I also saw a kangaroo with thorns like a porcupine and a beak. And Sam kept taking pics. After a while I took the phone away from him. I didn't want to drain its battery. I stopped trying to understand what the 'mixture' was after seeing an elephant with size of a rat and wings, maybe even horns above its ears.

Most of the creatures seemed venomous and sensitive to sound, but then again, I have no idea. I was only assuming this because this was my area of interest, forest, animals and travelling.

"Now, I'm tired." Chris said after a while. "We've been walking for ages now with nothing in sight"

I was still a little angry at him but let's be honest I couldn't stay angry forever.

"If you want, you can rest here in the middle of all these creatures" E-jay teased him.

That's when I heard some voices. I listened closely, and I could tell that they were speaking, and it was English, just in a very heavy accent. That was it! We found people; they could help us! I ran towards them before I could think.

"Where are you going?" E-jay asked while running behind me.

When I reached the voices, I realized that they weren't people, it was some human-fish-tiger creatures speaking in English. Great, it couldn't be people, it had to be one of these weird creatures. How did they speak English anyway? Whatever, I'm grateful because just talking in English made them almost human. They weren't mermaid-like-looking though, it was basically a fish with human legs and tiger paws. I wasn't surprised by anything anymore though.

"Hi." I said, my timid voice activated. "We need help, can you-"

"What's wrong with you?" E-jay whispered as he caught up, not knowing that I heard those Fish-Human-Tigers talk.

"Don't mind us." E-jay said to them while slowly trying to drag me out.

"E-jay" I whispered back. "They speak English."

The others came here now.

"What help do you want?" one of the fish-human-tigers asked and I realized that I could hardly understand their English at all, there accent was too hard.

"Can you tell us a way out of this island? Like, tell us if we could find-" "You are guest then." The other fish-human-tiger interrupted me.

"Is there a boat that could help us?" I said crossing my arms ignoring the other fish.

"Come with us." The second fish-human-tiger said ignoring me back. "We would be honored to show you our hospitality."

You know what it's getting really annoying to call them by such a long nick name. let's just call them Fihuti (**FI**sh-**HU**man-**TI**ger)

"No!" E-jay said. "I meant sorry but we were supposed to be in our house right now, all we really wanna do is reach home as soon as we can so can you just help us find a boat?"

Let me guess, he was freaking out by the idea of these things helping us.

"That's sad" the first one said. "We would have had really good food made fo-" "Really? I'm hungry!" Chris whispered loud enough for the whole world to hear.

After a 2 seconds awkward silence, Sam said just trying to cover up Chris, "We'd love to come"

Great. Now fishes will feed us. I sighed.

"Come, follow us then."

We followed them and walked till we reached a small cleared area where other Fihutis seemed to live.

It was an open area with hut-like structures made. It was just how a normal village would look but with Fihutis.

The two we had seen, talked to another Fihuti that I later found out was their king.

He welcomed us with open arms, a welcoming smile and asked us to stay for food. We *had* to say yes if we wanted to actually ask them about a boat.

They had a tradition since forever, I found out, in which the whole clan eats together. It was something that gave everyone a feeling of belongingness. It was sweet. The king Fihuti showed us the whole area introducing each and every person.

"This is Hirakanshumicha." He said.

"Hi" E-jay said. "Nice to meet you."

Such a long name. Wouldn't guess anyone's gender but the name sounded female.

"And this is Harakanjumaraman, her husband."

I was right then.

Dinner didn't take long enough too come.

Everyone slowly settled down. They were talking, laughing and were acting human. I had a *few* conversations myself. It was going so good till the *food* was served and I saw what we had to eat. Guess what *fishes* eat?

The *food* was made *of* algae *fresh* out *of* mud and rocks, mosses which had some insect gnawing it, LIVE-prawns, moving all across and some other ***GROSS*** things I couldn't even recognize. At this point, I wish there was a better word *for* gross but it looked really, really deadly. I wanted to puke. Make sure that you heard the word **LIVE**-prawns *correctly*.

"Ewwwww." I whispered. I paused and looked at Chris. "They say a really hungry person can eat anything. Let's see you eat this, Chris"

He passed a disgusted look.

"Sir?" Sam said looking at the king. "Can you tell us *if* there's a boat or something out there that would help us to pass the sea and get back to our place?"

"Son." He replied. "Why do you wanna go so early?"

Son?? Was there no other way for him to address my brother? And why won't we wanna go out of this weird island?

"We have to go back." Sam persisted trying to be as formal as possible. "Our parents are waiting for us."

I almost wanted to say, *do we look like we came to spend a vacation here?*

The King seemed disturbed for some reason.

"Finish your food before you go." He said as if he didn't even mean it.

"So, is there a boat?" I asked losing patience and not caring if I sounded rude.

He looked even more annoyed but answered anyway.

"People looking like you had come here before. They left their boat on the northern side of the island." He paused and then continued. "But it's almost night. You shouldn't leave a place that is alien to you at night."

I don't understand why they were trying to make us stay.

I sighed and looked back at my plate. I was **not** gonna eat whatever they asked me to at any cost. Not even a bite, I'd rather starve. I really would. I looked around and looked at jack who was next to me, lost in thoughts. I slowly took my bowl and put my food in Jack's bowl when he wasn't looking. I'm trying to believe how all the others ate it. Leaving the moving prawns, off course.

We were given a cottage -smaller than our caravan's bathroom- With ONE single bed to spend the night.

I didn't want to sleep. I don't think anyone did by the looks except, guess who, Chris, off course.

He slept on the bed while we were all silently looking at the wall waiting for the night to pass. Awkwardness creeping in all of us.

I never realized how big nights are till now. I was standing for like an hour, before I finally decided to roam around the place.

"The new travelers. They're pretty dumb, I believe."

Who just called us dumb? I looked at the cottage that was behind me and peeped through the window. It was the king and some other Fihuti. I don't know how I can differentiate the king with others, but I just can.

"You shouldn't have told them about the boat. They'll know where to run to." The other Fihuti said.

Why would we run? Okay, we could run, I mean, this place is trash but this was growing too sus at this point.

"And you also told them that people like them got it, what if they had asked about how they went back without their boat or why they didn't return back to where they came from?" That Fihuti continued.

Oh my god. There's something terribly wrong. I took a few steps back ready to run back to our cottage, still trying to listen more though.

"Anyway, I wish we could make them eat a little more food, get them fat. They'd be yummier that way. I've never tasted anyone tastier than those animals..."

I didn't even wait for the sentence to finish before running to our small cottage. I was breathing hard and was screaming at myself from the inside.

I mean, oh my god, how could I be so dumb? Why would they just wanna help us for no reason, anyway.

"Wake Chris up!" I screamed but not too loud as I reached inside our cottage. "Get out of here, they want to eat us."

"What?" E-jay asked half-sleepy.

"Chris!" I said ignoring E-jay's question. "I heard them talking about this."

"What *did* you hear?" Sam said.

"You know what, let's talk about it till they come here and eat us. GET. OUT!"

Finally, they all started to run out, Chris woke up and I had to practically push him out to make him start running. We ran and ran crossing the trees in the middle. I made sure to go on the opposite direction from where we came from. We were on the other side of the shore in not a long time while I was checking if anyone was behind us. I don't think they figured out that we had ran yet or maybe they did and thought we're long gone or... who cares, we got out, that's all. We got out and they weren't behind us.

I could hardly see anything and the dark wasn't helping either. But after a while, I could make out a boat, near to some trees on the shore where the forest cover was thicker, it was hidden and was in a very bad way. It looked really old, dusty but there were no holes in it so we put it on water and stepped on it. E-jay slid it through the grey ocean -yet again- and then got on. We decided to row turn by turn.

I sat down and looked at the island we just left. I had a funny thought. No matter how horrific to us today was, it had to be the coolest thing I ever did. I'd think about it for ages. Can't say the same about my brothers, they were shivering of fear.

We slowly rowed our way through the ocean and I felt a strange sense of relief, mostly for my brothers.

After a while the ocean seemed to have changed colours again. I can't exactly tell but I'm sure I can differentiate a metallic grey with night ocean colour. I've lived by the shore for far too long not to.

"I am gonna be honest, if this was an undiscovered island it's kinda weird that this grey ocean, all the mixed-up colours were not visible through any satellite." Sam said after a while.

"I told you; I think it's already discovered, just you don't know about it yet and maybe those creatures are just species we don't know of." I said. "Gimme your phone, E-jay."

"You have it." E-jay said.

I took it out and checked the compass on it.

"We're not going north." I said.

"Lemme check." Jack said.

I passed him the phone, and he dropped it. I didn't react instantly, I just rubbed my forehead and narrowed my eyes.

"Great!" I said sarcastically. "Now we have no idea at all where we're going, thanks a lot, Jack."

"Let's just turn a little and wish we're going the right way." Sam said. "E-jay, I think we should turn back and circle the outer ring of the grey ocean to reach back to the shore of the beach we came from."

"Wait, but look there." E-jay said pointing in a direction. "There's land, right there."

I looked in that direction and there *was* land. At this point, I felt there was something weird.

"But that's impossible, we won't even reach Antarctica this early." Sam said in disbelief.

"You're right" E-jay said, not knowing how to react.

It was impossible but let's be honest, this was the least *impossible* thing that happened in the whole day.

A Normaler Place

I wondered if I was actually dreaming. I've had weirder dreams lately, but this was too real. I couldn't believe this was happening, I doubted if we had actually found an unknown island or if this was actually just a dream.

As we went ahead, I saw a beach house on the shore, before even coming on it. We stopped at the beach and tied the boat to the shore. This place looked normal.

"Let's sleep in that beach house over there." I said. "If there's no one there."

"Honestly, I'd rather be reported to police than not sleep after all this." Chris said.

"You already slept." E-jay said. "So, *you're* gonna stay out and make sure no one's there."

Can't believe E-jay didn't ask us not to sleep there, that's what he'd usually do, but he looked like today was the day when he'd think of what's better for all of us rather than what's right. He,

I guess, just didn't want us to sleep on the ground. Of course, he didn't, we were all what people called golden spoon kids. We didn't know about how to live like this. Only now did I realize how serious this was. We could die of hunger here.

I think it's weird, what we're doing but we were desperate. As they say, desperate times call for desperate solutions. The next day we can ask any random person about where we are and stuff. There have to be people in *here*, right? Honestly, I don't know at this point, who knows, maybe this is a little more modern colony of Fihutis. I hope not. Even if so, I hope they have a phone, so that we can call our parents maybe. Plus, I'm terribly hungry right now. Although, if I got a chance to go back to when they were serving food, I still would've chosen not to eat it.

We went to the beach house and I quickly fell asleep. When I woke up, E-jay and Chris were arguing about who's the reason we're stuck here. It was annoying.

"Let me guess," I said more to myself while slowly going out of the beach house. "Chris slept which is obvious, you got angry, and instead of waking us up, started playing the blame game. You guys are so predictable. Grow up."

They stopped fighting and looked at me as I was on the gate.

"Do me a favor, and wake everyone up please." I said.

They woke Jack and Sam and were still rather a little angry on me.

"let's check if there's anyone in *this* place." E-jay said. "And no matter what happens, we stay together."

We nodded.

We walked a little and I saw a little puppy. As me, who personally hates dogs, I would've never been happier to see one. This gave a sign of normalcy. I still couldn't see people though.

"What's that?" Chris suddenly said. I turned back. I couldn't see anyone. "I'm pretty sure I saw someone there." He said pointing.

"It might be that dog." Sam said.

"But, it wasn't." Chris said.

"Sure" I said.

We walked a little more ignoring Chris' little prank, and talked about how exactly we reached that island and why it's weird that we've never heard of it. After we walked a little, I finally saw a glimpse normal living people, human beings, not fishes mixed with humans or spiders mixed with birds. It was humans, real humans, for half a second, I felt over the moon, and the other half second I realized...

Well, every person there was dressed in traditional old clothes of some country. I don't know which though.

"Why do I feel like people are dressed as 16th century, Germany?" Sam said.

Okay, that answers my question. Now, this was so not what I expected, but now we know, I can't find a phone to call mom or dad. Although, for the record, this is a way normaler place compared to the ones we've seen before. We walked around a little more and found a place to sit.

"Wow." Sam said sarcastically. "Can you believe it? What's going on? At this point, I'm questioning my existence."

"I'm questioning your existence, each day, so let's not talk about it." Chris said. This felt more like Chris, than it had all the time here.

"So, you're he one to talk, huh." Sam said referring to how he had crashed us here.

"I think we've time travelled." I said sitting down, more to myself (unknowingly stopping a fight from happening). "I don't know how but that would explain a lot of things, like this place, maybe we time-travelled to Germany and the island was destroyed with time or something."

"Maybe" Sam said. "But it still would be weird that we've never even heard of such stories. Isn't that what legends are made of?"

"Who knows?" I said in a think-about-it way. "Maybe, there are legends about this place in Germany."

"Ok, how exactly do you think we have time travelled?" E-jay said.

"Oh my god!" Someone said from behind us before I could answer. "Are you kidding me?"

We turned. It was a girl around sixteen. A little more than round face, blonde hairs with one of the prettiest blue eyes I've ever seen. For a second, I thought she heard us, and she thought of us as time-travelers and got amazed or something.

"Is it so hard to understand you're on a different planet?" She said.

Crasioda

"Who are you?" I said sharply.

"Oh yeah, I'm sorry." "Nice to meet you, sorry." Sam suddenly interrupted, **trying** be funny. No one laughed.

"Oh-k" she said awkwardly. "I'm Emma."

"And?" I said. "Who told you, you're allowed to listen to people's private conversations?"

She smirked which made me narrow my eyes and said, "Who told **you**, that you can sleep in *my* beach house?"

That shut me up. But, I kinda had a bad feeling about her.

"Anyway," she said. "You wanna how you're actually here?"

"Bro, what? How would you know?" I asked her sharply, again.

"Because," she said. "I know a lot about Earth. I knew that just yesterday a warm hole between Earth and Crasioda had opened. I wasn't expecting anyone to come though, I mean there's only like a trillion to one chance that anyone would come in the ten minutes that the warm hole is open."

"So, you know more about Earth than the people living in it, ok." I said sarcastically not too loud. Then:

"Wait. We're not on earth?"

"Why are you acting so rude?" Sam whispered.

I signed. I won't be surprised if she ends up stealing our things or something while tricking us into a weird story. Emma was about to answer me when:

"So, Emma, right?" Sam said. "I'm Sam."

"I caught all of your names while I was" "Following us?" Chris suddenly said in a I-knew-it way. "I told you there was someone behind us."

"You were following us?" E-jay asked who looked like the only one as creeped out as me by the situation. Chris, on the other hand looked like he was proud to prove he wasn't lying, as if it was supposed to be normal.

"Kinda" Emma said. "But like that's because you're celebrities to me. Seeing Earthians *for* real! I *feel* starstruck."

I looked at Chris who gave another, I'm-just-so-cool expressions *be*fore saying, "You sound like we're in a boy group called Earth and you're our *fangirl*."

"Okay, I know it's a little creepy but I'll start *from* the start, okay?" she said.

"Okay" Sam said interested.

"So, you're on Crasioda and I always loved to explore outer space. Always did. But your planet Earth," She continued still sounding like a *fangirl* describing her *fav*orite boy group. "It's one which I *find* really cool. It has way lesser species as compared to any planet I've ever known and humans seem to be the superior power everywhere, it's so similar to my own planet." "I'm sorry, what?" Chris said. "How's this planet similar to Earth?"

"Well," she said kind *of* realizing interruptions will simply have to be there. "Our planet also lives by Oxygen, has gravity, has water more than land, has a magnetic *field* around it, ozone layer too..." I think I lost her after magnetic field, she kept saying things that are common between the 2 planets, and at a point she started using too much scientific language and I seriously couldn't understand her.

"Are you done?" I finally said. "We get it, you love Earth. Get to the point."

"Okay" she said. "So, I knew about when the next warm hole will form and all that. I don't even know why I collect this information but it proved to be useful. Then I went to my beach house to see 5 strangers sleeping in it. I almost called the royal guards till I looked at your 'Earthy' clothes. I knew that instant, you guys were from Earth."

I honestly wanted to know how she knew about Earth at all, but then I was like who cares?

"Warm holes? How did our scientist not know about it?" Sam said after a long silence.

"Because you guys don't believe, any other alien could exist unless in science-fiction."

She took two pieces of paper out of her small bag and made one dot on one, and a large circle on the other.

"Ok" she said. "The small dot is Earth and the bigger one is Crasioda, the papers are the respective universes and rest everything is outer space. When the two universes overlap and our planets come under each other, a small meeting of atmospheres cause warm holes and that's how you came here. Got it?"

No one had asked how warm holes are formed. Even though I found it cool, no one asked.

"Not really." Chris said.

She explained the same thing again.

"You know like a connect was formed."

"I don't understand." Chris said.

She explained again.

"I'm not your teacher so I don't care." She said after she had explained for the fifth time.

"Anyway." She said finally giving up. "So, here's the deal that I had thought of. I'll help you get back to Earth and you answer some of my questions, ok?"

Questions and Answers

To be honest, I still don't trust her, I don't even think she's saying the truth about us being on another planet, but even if there's a slightest chance of whatever she's saying could be true, then I'd like to hold on to it.

She asked us to stay in her place for a day before starting to move.

"How exactly are you planning to help us out?" I asked.

"There's a spaceship" Emma said. "I sneak in it frequently to visit Earth."

That answered my question about how she knew about Earth.

I just realized now that she had a smile on her face all the time, and walked almost musically like she was always on her happiest.

"Sneak?" Sam asked. "You mean it's not yours?"

"Not really." Emma replied. "But whoever owns it hasn't showed up to take it back. It was because of the spaceship that I could ever visit Earth or anywhere else."

"That's still basically stealing." E-jay whispered to me.

"Is it?" Emma asked in a way saying 'I heard that' while flipping her golden locks.

We reached her house.

"Won't your parents mind?" Sam asked.

"My parents?" Emma replied. "There're...uh... out for a few days so I'm home alone."

She was nowhere older than 18, so no way she was living alone. There was something sus about the way she said that. Plus, it's weird how her parents had gone somewhere *just* when we came here. Coincidence? I think not. She's hiding something. Although, no one else even seemed to question that.

"Ok." Emma said. "So, these questions would make people from your planet understand that I'm not from there so I never asked anything while I was on Earth, but now that you're the aliens, tell me who's the keeper of your planet? How exactly was your world formed, and what's with everyone's weird addiction with phones?"

"Phones?" Sam asked.

"That's not an addiction to anyone." Chris said. "Phones are important."

"Ok" she said. "Tell me about how the world is formed"

Sam's face beamed because someone finally gave him a chance to talk about all these boring things. It took him two seconds to turn the next hour into a science class, Sam somehow went from explaining her the creation of the world to the creation of the laws of motion, then on how the dinosaurs died and before I knew it, they were talking about atoms, cells, physics, even geography at one point. Then, she started talking about how her planet is even bigger than our sun. To be honest, this conversation wouldn't have been this boring if 2 nerds weren't using all the scientific words that could ever exist. It's safe to say that almost everyone lost interest; except Sam, that is.

“Anyway, what do you mean by keeper?” I heard Sam. Can’t believe they were still talking; I almost fell asleep. “You were asking about it.”

“The keeper of magic.” Emma replied as if it was the most obvious thing in the world. Sam paused, probably shocked, but to be honest, nothing was shocking me anymore.

I shrugged and said, “Maybe there’s no magic on Earth.”

“That’s not possible.” Emma said with a laugh. “If Earth has life, it has to have magic, and a keeper.”

“There’s no magic, whatsoever, at least not on Earth.” I said very casually. Although kinda waiting for her to prove me wrong. “Or else something like school wouldn’t have been invented.”

She gave me a no-way-that’s-true look and got up. She went somewhere and got a ..... laptop?

“These things sell here?” Sam asked before I could.

“No” she said. “I got it the last time I went to outer space.”

“It needs internet to work.” I said.

"Mine doesn't." She said. She opened the laptop and opened YouTube. The *fact* that it opened was enough *proof* that she wasn't lying. "This isn't an Earthy laptop, it is *from* another planet, *that* isn't unaware *of* the *fact* that they are not alone in the universe."

I *felt* badly *offended*. "We know we're not alone in the world." I said angrily even though that was a lie. I probably never even thought what was beyond Earth. "We just didn't know, who else was there."

"Whatever." She said while searching on it about our magic.

"There!" She said when a video titled, 'Earth's magic' came up.

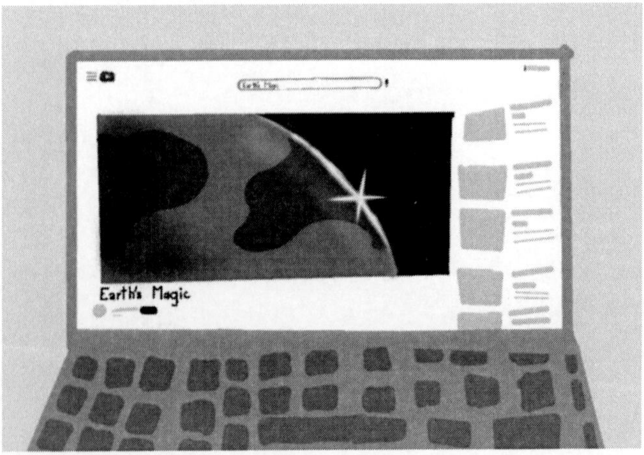

"Earthians are so wound up in their own life that they hardly ever try to dive deeper in the what and why part. I mean I tried to find answers of so many questions by listening to people talk on Earth, but no one would ever get over talking about themselves"

"I'm sorry, what?" E-jay said, just as offended from behind me. I only, then, realized that all my brothers were looking at the laptop.

"Don't get offended." She said very casually. "That's the same with my planet too, okay? I'm the only geek, who tries to explore the outside world too. Just that people at least know other stuff exists" She paused and then said, "Although, I still can't believe you don't know who your keeper is. That's like common sense in everywhere."

I sighed.

Can we stop this conversation already?

"What is a keeper?" Sam finally asked.

"Well," she said. "That is the one person who makes sure that life on the planet will not end after just a few million years later, say in Earth, the keeper keeps the core rotating so that gravity stays intact. *And*, he or she does that using magic."

"Ok." I said. "Why don't you search up who our keeper is on this laptop."

"Hey," Emma said. "planet's keepers are not revealed on the internet, it's dangerous to reveal it to everyone; you know, like how queens never reveal their most irresistible food, so that no one can poison them."

A smile crossed my face, and I started laughing on this weird idea.

"People actually do that? Who is this queen!?" I said still laughing.

"I know, right?" she said.

I was still giggling.

"She'd be insane" I said.

"You don't even know her." She said suddenly serious for no reason.

I stopped.

"Whatever." E-jay said rather irritated. "Can you take us to your spaceship, if you're done with all your questions."

"What's the hurry?" Emma asked while getting up.

"The fact that our parents would be looking for us all over the planet, and guess what? We're not on the planet." He said not in his usual 'all is well' self.

"Ok, let's go" she said with a numb, angry face.

Ok, usually I'd be the one showing this behavior. I guess, he was just pissed by the fact that we were here wasting our time when mom and dad might be worried sick. It was true, I could only imagine how scared they might be. I know they'd be looking over everywhere. I'm sure they'd readily searched all of

Australia. They probably wouldn't even think of going beyond there. Meanwhile, we are not only outside the country, or planet or solar system but outside the whole universe.

Walking to the spaceship

We got up and Emma angrily took some stuff in a small basket. Guess she really wanted to keep going with the whole keeper thing.

We walked through the busy market to a lonely path. As we walked on, we found ourselves in a forest. All the while Emma didn't speak a word.

After walking a little, I looked up. I found a big cloud-like looking fog, it was filled beautifully with different colors. something about it, though just seemed majestical. It was as if someone painted cotton candy in many colors and sent it to the sky. It looked designed, almost crafted perfectly and magnificently. I felt hypnotized, somehow.

This place might be weird but it's still really beautiful. This sort of reminded me of that randomly colored island, it may have been scary, but there's no way I could ever forget it, can I? This planet really was wonderful, I remember when I overheard Emma saying that Crasioda, had way more than a hundred times Earth's a few million species and that almost no one knows what type of animal they'd find in the very next city. That gives you so many things to explore, to find, and too many places ready to be found. I don't think that could happen on Earth. I mean, we know everything, maybe not everything but practically everything. You never run upon something pretty, you hear about it and find it. Now that I think about it, this is because humans are everywhere and all the different species are packed in a few corners. You can't run upon any species randomly because the population of human itself is so much more than number of species on Earth.

Wait, I never felt that before... I always thought that my own planet itself is too big to explore in one life, now when I know that there are planets as big as Crasioda exists, Earth just suddenly feels ... too small. I think this is the type of place I'd love to live in. A place where you have no idea what's next and every day is an adventure.

"Ok, I'm tired. Let's stop here for a while." Emma said. It was only now that I realized that everyone was having another conversation and Emma seemed to be back to her usual self.

Lost

After walking for a while, we stopped between a big apple tree garden. I looked up at the sky. That cloud wasn't there anymore.

I sat down under the shadow of one of the apple trees. Ah... this place is so amazing and different, at this point why do I even wanna return. *For mom and dad and friends,* I told myself. *They're still on Earth.* I really wish I could borrow that spaceship that Emma would show us or something like that, so that I could come back here sometimes.

I actually trust Emma now. I don't know why, but I guess she can't be in the 'stranger danger' zone if she's not a stranger anymore. I don't know why I'm getting so addicted to this place, I mean, I'm sure if I was born here, I'd find it just like Earth.

"Do you have some food?" Jack asked popping my bubble of imagination.

"Do I look like a food machine to you?" I replied irritated that he interrupted my thoughts.

He paused for sec, then replied, "You could have been nice about it."

"How do you expect me to have food, huh? Ask Emma, she has that big basket with her."

He looked towards her and then said, “Why don’t you like her? She’s only been nice to us.”

I felt pissed at this comment because Sam had been saying this all day long and I didn’t want to explain my trust issues again. I especially didn’t want to discuss my sudden change of opinion about her. I mean, explaining to Sam is one thing, repeating it to everyone was another.

“I’ll hate anyone I want to and have all the trust issues in the world. What’s your problem?”

He didn’t say anything, looked down and just went towards Emma. Ok, now I felt bad. I didn’t mean to be rude. Whatever, he’ll forget it in an instant.

I later saw him take an apple from one of the trees so I guess he didn’t mind.

After a while everyone found a corner and sat. I fell asleep. It was all so tiring.

*****

It was around a little later when E-jay woke me up as if the world was ending and screamed, "Get up!"

"What is it?" I asked still half asleep.

"Jack's lost."

The fight

I forgot everything else and asked, "What? Where did you last see him?"

"Right there." He said pointing to one of the apple trees. "I remember looking at him and the next second he was just gone."

"How could you be so careless?" I screamed.

"Can you get mad later and find him?"

I sighed, sure, ignore the topic! I looked around the apple tree to find a clue or something. I didn't find anything but a half-eaten apple that was turning black.

Something was wrong.

I looked in other places. All of us were looking for him and everyone was panicked. All of us except Emma. I seriously almost felt like I was overreacting about her. I almost felt I was wrong, but now I feel she *is* doing something fishy. A thought crossed in my mind. What if she's like a scientist researching on aliens? Trying to get DNA and stuff from test subjects?

Stop it. I told myself, now's not the time.

"What if he's on the tree." Chris said as we were trying to find Jack.

"He's not as dumb as you to climb up a tree and not come down while we're looking and screaming for him. Besides, he can't even climb."

"Let's still try."

"Can you seriously, just use your brain at least to find Jack, please, I'm begging you!"

"Well, maybe you would've seen him if you didn't sleep."

"And maybe none of this would've happened at all if you simply didn't drive! I mean how could you possibly confuse break and an accelerator? Even I know the difference!"

"You don't even know what happened! Someone had just passed the road too suddenly; I couldn't control the steering. I panicked. Everyone screaming didn't help either! I pressed the break just to realize it wasn't a break at all. Do you think I don't feel guilty at all for this. Like I legit think this is a joke? I'm scared like all of you."

I paused as I saw him gulp a heavy breath down his throat.

"Maybe I wouldn't even have drove if you wouldn't have made the comment about me never learning how to drive."

"Well, you did prove me right, you know." I said ending the conversation right there.

I turned my vision away from him just to see Emma sharpening a wooden stick by a rock. What was she doing? That could hurt someone. Maybe that's exactly what she's trying to do. Maybe this was the plan all along, gain their trust, make one of them a lab test subject and give everyone else a sober goodbye.

I couldn't let her do this. And I'm going to find my brother. I went up to her and asked, "Can you show that thing to me, just for a second."

She gave me weird look but still let me have the stick. I looked at it for a while and then, put that stick under her neck like a knife.

"What did you do to my brother?" I screamed. I was acting crazy and I knew it but this might just end up saving us.

"Are you insane?!!!" She screamed.

"I can do anything for my brothers. Don't. Test. Me. Let me guess, this was your plan to kidnap my brother, send him to your parents and make him a test subject on DNA test or something, huh? That's why you never talked about your parents?"

She tried to push me away looking hurt.

"You don't know anything about my parents."

"What are you doing?" Chris said trying to yank me off. I pushed him away and said, "She has done something, why else would she be so relaxed in such a serious situation?"

E-jay heard us by then and pulled me off with Chris' help.

"Are you insane?" E-jay said holding both my shoulders tight so I don't run off. But my focus wasn't here, my focus was on Emma. She almost had tears but then she ran away from us. Emma ran off, either because she was scared of me or because she thought I figured out what she was doing.

“I’m sorry” I said. “But there’s a big chance she has something to do with it. You know like they show in movies, scientist wanting to test aliens. We’re the aliens.”

Another tree

E-jay let go of me. That's when I saw Sam running towards us.

"What did you do?" He said to me. "I saw her running off almost crying."

"I wasn't trying to hurt her." I said. "It was just to scare her into saying the truth."

"You also blew our only chance to get home"

"Is it that or do you just already miss your nerd friend?"

"Stop it!" E-jay screamed at me. "It's a different thing to not trust someone and a different thing to try to stab them"

"You did WHAT?" Sam looked at me, eyes so wide, they could pop out.

I couldn't handle this. I thought E-jay was on my side when it came to not trusting Emma. I know what I did was kinda scary, but he could understand my emotions on it, they can't really think, I would hurt her, but here they were, doing exactly that.

I pushed everyone aside and ran towards the midst of the apple trees.

"*Where are you going??*"E-jay screamed from behind me.

"Trying to find Jack that side. What do you think?" I said while still running.

I stopped in front of a tree and looked at it, sat under it. I felt something was wrong with how it was going. I wasted so much of my time fighting everyone that I could've used to find Jack. I'm pretty sure, I could've done something different than pissing everyone off, this is how far my anger issues got me. That's how it's always been. Me trying to fix everything just to ruin it. This was my every time. Who knows where Jack is? Did he get angry because of me? It is my fault. Like always. Chris got offended and drove us into an accident because of me. I gave E-jay a hard time on everything. Jack got angry because of me. Everything, *everything* was my fault. "I'm so stupid." I murmured.

"You are stupid." I heard a deathly cold voice, echoing in my ears and glanced up and backed away from the tree a little. It was... a talking shadow?

"How could stabbing anyone solve your problem. You weirdo."

I chuckled mockingly and said, "I definitely believe a shadow, who can't even do something like that."

"Guess then you won't believe that I know where your brother is, either."

"I won't. I have trust issues."

"Your brother told me about Mark." He paused. Then "And what's wrong with being a shadow?"

I stared at it. Jack had told me that Mark. A secret between just us. Mark used to bully him. Even the rest of my brothers didn't know about this. This was between us. I had scared that kid off around a year ago, told him to stay away from Jack. If the shadow isn't lying, why would Jack bring him up again?

"Where is he?" I asked.

He just smirked and clapped with his hands (no sound came) and poof! we were somewhere else now.

How Jack's mind works

I opened my eyes and looked in front of me. It looked like a wall made of strange gel. I heard a faint female singing voice growing louder -just enough to hear it properly- with each second. That voice was just beautiful and hypnotizing. It was in a different language but I could make out some English, somehow. It was as if that voice was calling me from the other side of the wall. I tried to put my finger in it and that very second I heard the word 'blue' from the voice then suddenly the whole wall turned blue and I found myself going in the blue gel-ish thingy, completely hypnotized.

The voice stopped as soon as I entered. I could see a whole new world around me. Everything was black and there were many clusters of blue threads which were glowing. Each and everything were projecting something, memories.

All of these memories were blue. I saw a memory of Mark pushing Jack and Jack betraying no emotion on his face, another one of Jack crying in a corner. I walked ahead and saw a small yellow spot in that big blue ocean-ish thingy. It was of when we were sitting in the restaurant and me and Sam were arguing about not letting Chris drive; when Jack supported Chris and I told him to let us do the talking, was I that rude? Suddenly, the memory turned blue. I didn't even remember this happening. Now that I think about it, I sounded as if I was rejecting him from family discussion. I looked around and saw the time when I scared Mark away from Jack, it was yellow and Jack seemed really happy. I remembered that but I didn't remember me telling him that he was so weak for not fighting for himself. This was another yellow memory that turned blue. I never felt this guilty about anything ever. As I walked more I saw a memory of Mark troubling him asking him to go crying back to his older sister. Jack never told me about it. But why? Because he wanted to fight this himself, the way I told him to. I felt so toxic. I felt like an older sister who only makes the main character feel worse than he/she already is. I didn't want to go more ahead. I just didn't.

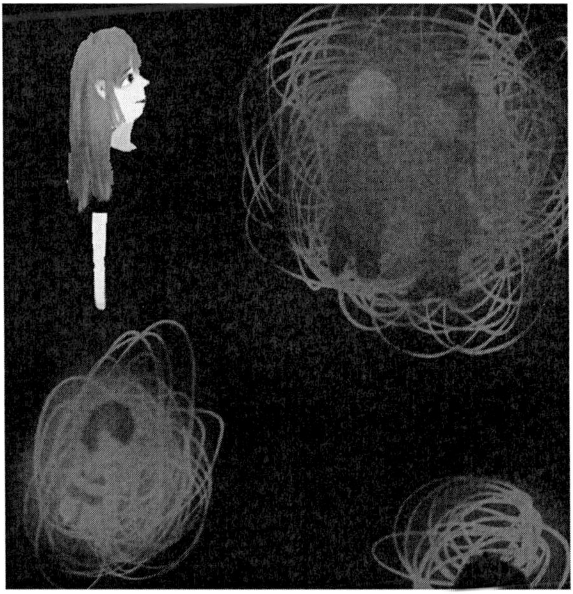

I felt terrible.

"Woah!" I said. I opened my eyes. I wasn't in Jack's brain anymore. I was on a chair and I could see some hair-like threads going away from my brain, to a prison where I saw Jack, sleeping unconsciously.

"How did you feel?" said someone's cold voice as I jumped. It was the same shadow, the same one that took me here.

"You know your brother's been so sad lately all because of you." He said in the same deathly cold voice, came around me and gave an evil smile. Not that it made me scared.

"Why do you care?" I asked.

"Just trying to make you feel more guilty about his death."

What? I ...... felt numb. D-d-did he just say that ... he killed my brother. I forgot how to speak for a while. He was too young to die. No, there's no way, right? Seconds passed as I looked at the cage again, he wasn't sleeping. He was........*dead.* I couldn't move or speak. I was completely numb.

"Why?" I finally managed to say in a low whisper.

"Oh, he's not dead yet." He said casually.

Ok, I felt back to my bones again.

"Sounds like you want something." I said angry. "What is it?"

"Clever. I want you to kill someone."

As if.

"Umm, no, pretty sure, you can do that yourself."

"So, the deal is, I'm a lost soul and to actually live normally I need someone else's freshly dead body, that is someone who died just 0.03 seconds ago. That could be your brother, but... I'm greedy and I want to kill a wizard."

"You want me to kill a wizard for you? Are you insane?"

"Don't" He said. "interrupt me again ever again." He looked at me and continued "That's why I invented poisonous apple, which put humans in deep sleep and kill wizards, in a while depending on how strong that wizard is, while replacing their soul with me. Although, wizards in here are too smart and I've given up trying with them, they don't fall for it at all. I just want you to press this button" He pointed at a button on a wall. "and these poisonous apples will reach Earth, because Earth's wizards are really clueless compared to us mostly because, to them, these apples are just stories."

"Why won't you just do that yourself? and what if a non-wizard eats it?"

"You don't worry about that. I'm not gonna let my only chance go. Now, I can't send it because dark magic things can only be sent to a different planet by that planet's citizen. So, all you have to do is press that button over there."- he pointed at the brown rusted button again- "And you can take your brother back. He's unconscious and pretty useless to me."

Ok. To me it doesn't sound so big. If E-jay would be here, he would've tried to find a different deal all together, because "We can't be the reason for someone's death". So thankful he's not here do use this stupid decision. Honestly, I don't think pressing a button would make me a murder, right? Plus, my brother is definitely more important than any other random person who's actually a wizard. Right?

"My brother ate a poison apple? How'll he wake up? No true love kisses, whatever, right?" I suddenly asked.

"That could be an option but I can undo the spell after you press the button."

There we go again

How bad could it be? I know I'm being selfish but a single tsunami kills thousands of people, would a single person really matter. I think I'm doing it.

"Ok." I said. "But you'll wake Jack up first. I have nowhere to run, but you can just deny any time, right? So, wake him up."

"Ok." He agreed.

He looked on his right side. I saw Jack there again.

He snapped his fingers.

"Done."

"Nothing magical-looking happened." I said. But almost instantly I saw Jack opening his eyes slowly.

I didn't say anything. I looked at the rusty old button and pressed it before I could convince myself otherwise. Again, nothing magical-looking happened. But, I know something else would have happened.

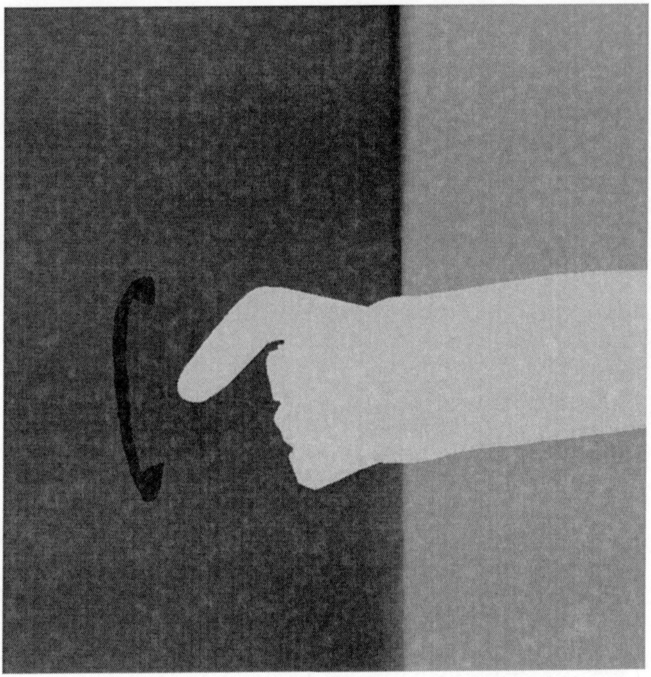

“What’s going on?” I heard Jack.

“Jack!” I ran to him inside the prison, closed my eyes and hugged him tight, also realizing that I hadn’t hugged him in the last 10000 years.

When I opened my eyes, I was back in between the apple trees.

“What happened to me?” Jack asked. “The last thing I remember is having an apple, then I felt sleepy and then I saw you in the dark room and your shadow looked weird and” “Just tell the others I saved you; I'll *flex* it on you *for* the rest *of* my life."

"You did?"

"Yes! I had to *fight* monsters and *stuff for* you, you can almost call me your savior."

"The *fact* that I can't even say 'as *if*'. Guess I'll *just* believe you."

Going back

"Sally!" I heard Sam scream as we walked back.

"Wait! That's Jack!" that was Chris.

"Are you guys okay?" E-jay started. "I mean what were you even thinking?! Are you completely out of your mind...." Then, he went on and on about how insane I was about trying to stab Emma, and how I shouldn't have gone that far in there and... well, I'm gonna save you the pain of listening to his ten-hour lecture.

"but" he finally said. "I'm just glad you guys are ok. How did you find jack anyway?"

I just smiled. "I'll tell you guys later, ok?"

"Can we go home now, where's Emma?" Jack said.

"Yeah," Sam said looking at me. "Where is she, Sally?"

Well, I'll be very honest, I can't control myself when I'm angry, ok? But honestly, now I really feel bad, I think I even want to say sorry, but I guess she won't be coming, I feel wrong, honestly, I do.

Sam was still looking at me, then rolled his eyes and said, "Well, but while trying to find you guys we did find the spaceship she was talking about, so..."

"You did?" I said.

"Yeah" E-jay said. "And you guys have a lot of explaining to do when we go in."

As we walked towards the spaceship I realized that it wasn't as far from us as I expected. We reached there in just a few minutes.

"Sam, you sure you can drive it?" Chris asked when we went in.

"How hard can it be?" Sam replied.

Well turns out it was *really* hard with around 100000000 buttons to understand. Luckily, Sam found a guidebook... which was thick the size of a tree. Plus, Sam had a 'we can't leave until everything's figured out' attitude so it pretty much felt like days had passed by the time he had read all the pages.

"Ok" Sam finally said. "let's go, sit down put your seatbelt as tight as you possibly can."

I did that. He started the spaceship. Then I felt the shuttle go up and suddenly I felt myself being pushed towards my seat as if I was to merge with it, also a continues whooooooosh sound was in everyone's ears. The speed did nothing but increase and I felt I could very make a hole in my seat and fall behind it until suddenly it became slow and steady.

"You can lower your seatbelts now... if you're not afraid of flying into another dimension. Just kidding, you can get up." Sam said.

Chris was the first one to get up, he looked at the screen. I couldn't even manage to move, though.

"Why does it show it'll take us 3 Earth years to reach Earth." Chris asked.

"We're lucky that we're close to the planet or it would have taken us centuries." Sam said.

Do I really need to explain what I feel right now. My eyes were just wide. I couldn't even find words at this point.

"What's this?" Chris said. "It says hyper speed."

"In the guidebook they said it will make us reach Earth in at most 5 sec but theories say that it is very risky, the smallest deviation in path can cause us to reach a different universe all together, so stay away from that button." Sam warned.

"Are you insane?" Chris said pressing the button without thinking anything.

That very second I felt the same pull with my seat but much, *much* stronger. Luckily no one had opened their seatbelts except Chris who got pushed on his seat (just in an awkward position) for the longest 5 seconds of his life as far as I know and then the shuttle just stopped.

When we opened the door, well, all I'll say is we definitely were *not* on Earth......